THE BIG O SHOW

Jon Lange

Copyright © 2014 Jon Lange

All rights reserved.

DEDICATION

This is dedicated to all those people who rejected my idea.
You know who you are.

CONTENTS

Preface

This was originally published by me in a very limited edition in the summer of 2000 as a proposal for a new programme idea I wanted to sell to television production companies. It was rejected by all of them, including the ones working on behalf of major channels like Channel 4 and Channel 5 here in the UK. I was quite surprised at Channel 4's refusal to even consider the idea as I believed it would be right up their street, considering it was the more radical out of all the terrestrial channels. Remember, this was the channel that broadcasted for the first time such controversial films as Kubrick's *A Clockwork Orange,* Ken Russell's *The Devils*, and Friedkin's *The Exorcist*, so I fail to comprehend why my little idea did not match their 'criteria.'

I should explain that I had stopped watching television for about ten years. Having gone through a difficult separation and now finding myself single again, the last thing I wanted to do was stay in and watch crummy TV. All I wanted to do at the time was go out and enjoy myself, have a few beers, and play around, whilst I was still young enough. But after ten years even that got boring, so I started watching TV again. I was quite surprised at the content of some of the programmes being aired, and Channel 5 was showing some excellent programmes. I remember one was called 'G-String Girls' which showed plenty of nudity. I quite liked that programme, as well as the films they used to show on Fridays late at night (amusingly referred to as T & A films). There was also a series presented by the delectable Eden called 'OutThere,' with clips from obscure, independent films, with lots of weird scenes and plenty of nudity on display as well. It was always a pleasure to watch. What happened to it? And why was the series cancelled?

But I remember thinking at the time, 'Wow! This is what I've been missing out on!'

Even Channel 4 did not disappoint. I fondly remember on Saturday nights they had a series called 'Karaoke Fish' (I think) which was very different, and an unusual idea (a fish presenting music in a fish tank, with lots of montages extracted from some wonderful films as the music played). They also had a series called 'Disinformation' about subversive culture, featuring underground spokesmen like Alan Moore, Grant Morris, Genesis P. Orridge, and other interesting people. They also had an enlightening series on obscure European films called 'Mondo Macabro' scripted by Pete Tombs, an expert in that field, featuring interviews with alternative filmmakers like Jess Franco, Jean Rollin, José Larraz, etc. And there was a DVD review series called 'Vids' hosted by two foul-mouthed lads who would use rather coarse language when reviewing the latest releases (I distinctly remember one review being carried out whilst the presenter was busy on the toilet).

So I still fail to understand why my idea was rejected.

But over the last 10-15 years terrestrial television, I am afraid to say, has become rather dull. Only occasionally do we get the odd programme that may be worth watching. I remember the announcement of a series called 'Bad Culture' on Channel 4 which was going to be presented by the art critic Matthew Collings. I was looking forward to it as I had known some of the participants involved and therefore couldn't wait to see them on television. When it was eventually aired I was very disappointed as Mr Collings appeared not to have done his homework at all. His interview with the industrial band Coil was embarrassing to say the least. But what really got me was the amount he was paid; about £200,000. I could have come up with something ten times better for half the fee. Similarly, there was a programme about the *Kama Sutra* on Channel 4 presented by the Asian 'comedian' (I use that word reluctantly) Sanjeev Bhaskar. As I started watching it, it soon became apparent that this programme wasn't about the book itself; it had more to do with Mr Bhaskar's ignorance of the subject. So my verdict on that programme was that it was a complete waste of time and Channel 4's money. But at least Mr Bhaskar got a free trip to India out of it!

The only thing that has been on recently, and was worth watching, was Channel 4's live screening of an autopsy, performed by Dr Gunther von Hagens (*Autopsy: Life and Death*) in 2006. Since then they have shown nothing controversial to mark out it as being the radical channel that it used to be. It has become rather stale, and even the films it has been showing lately have been somewhat bland. So I think it's about time Channel 4 performed an autopsy on itself to discover why, if at all possible, over the years it has become such a boring channel.

So what is wrong with television today? Why is it so bloody boring? Why don't they have anything interesting on anymore?

That brings me to my little idea. It is for the above reasons that I am publishing it again; I still believe it would have made a very interesting programme. By making it available to everyone, rather than just prospective production companies, you can now judge for yourself.

When it was originally published as a small pamphlet there was no proper preface or an explanation of what the programme was all about. I thought it would be expedient to omit a long explanatory introduction and left it up to the judgement of the readers, basing their opinion on the prototype of the script I provided. It may be for this reason that it was possibly rejected, simply because they failed to understand it. I have therefore decided to include here a short preliminary discourse in the hope that this will be enlightening so that the script can be read in the right frame of mind. Perhaps then it will make more sense to everyone.

My programme is all to do with sex. Actually, it is more to do with the most intimate experience a couple can share together; an orgasm (the big 'O' of the show). But there is no penetration involved, there is no touching, there is no nudity; just gold old healthy orgasms being produced in people by a technique little known here in the West, and very similar to what Christians term 'laying on of hands.'

In the East such techniques as the one I am describing here have been used for thousands of years. They usually involve the manipulation of subtle energy in the human body through subtle nerve channels and getting this energy to flow properly. Thus you find it in acupuncture where it is manipulated by the use of needles. It is also found in Ayurveda. In that practise this subtle energy is called *ojas*, a term I have adopted simply because it has magical connotations, and sounds interesting. I could have used the term *prana*, as that is indeed identical, but it just sounds boring, and most people have heard of it, especially if they know anything about yoga. It is exactly the same as *ojas*; it is the subtle energy that vitalises the nerves and gives them energy. Similarly, by manipulating *prana*, which is done through various contortions of the body in yoga, we are able to get it to flow more naturally. Many illnesses are attributed to the blocking of this energy, resulting in mental and physical disorders like rheumatism, arthritis, and even neuroses.

Ojas, a Sanskrit word, literally means *vigour*. In the principles of Ayurveda, it is the essential energy of the body, and can be equated with the *fluid of life*. Practitioners of Ayurveda say it is the 'sap of one's life energy.' When it is sufficient in the body our immunity system is working properly. When it is deficient, our immunity is weakened resulting in fatigue, stress, and ultimately disease. Like Macrobiotics, there is a whole system behind it, including a correct and healthy diet, to ensure that this energy is never depleted, and makes for a better and healthier lifestyle.

Ojas is the purest substance in the universe when it is flowing properly. It is omnipresent in the human body and is responsible for higher states of consciousness, including purity of thoughts, perfect health, positive feelings like love, joy, etc. When we experience a higher state of consciousness the flow of *ojas* increases, or rather we experience a higher state of consciousness because it is at its maximum. It reaches its maximum output at the point of orgasm. In fact, an orgasm is the result of *ojas* 'overflowing,' and it is this overflowing which gives us the sense of peace, calmness and contentment that we experience after sex. In other words, it reaches its fruition by flowing between the two poles of masculine and feminine. When these two poles converge in sex there is a mutual exchange of *ojas*, giving the pleasurable sensation of an orgasm. If orgasm is lacking in sex, then it means that *ojas* is not flowing properly and that no mutual exchange has taken place. Hence there is an anti-climax. By practising certain disciplines it is possible to control the flow of *ojas* and to get it to reach its highest level of output so that both parties experience orgasm at the same time.

In Tantra there is a similar type of energy known as *kundalini*. This is likened to a serpent coiled up at the base of the spine (i.e. as potential energy). During sex this energy is awakened and comes into play and vitalises the genitals, making them active. When a man starts to ejaculate it is the *kundalini* that is forcing the prostrate gland to expand and start pumping the gleet to get the sperm moving. *Kundalini* is then visible as an outer manifestation, i.e. the semen. For women, the outer manifestation of *kundalini* during sexual arousal is the vaginal secretions.

Those who are experts in working with *kundalini* can experience an orgasm themselves by awakening it at the base of the spine and taking it all the way up the spine through the subtle nerve centres (or *chakras*) and getting it to flow through the back of the head and out through the subtle aperture at the top of the skull. I have done this personally many times, and the result is probably about the most powerful orgasm you could ever experience. Some prefer to call it a 'mystical union,' or 'union with the goddess,' or many other mystical terms. But as there is an accompanying arousal of the genitals, with a perfect erection, then this has to be sex at its best, since you are not making love with a partner; you are making love with the universe.

Those who have worked with *kundalini* can also help others to experience it by arousing it in them and then transmitting that energy to the *chakras* of their partners. They in turn will feel the sleeping serpent awaken, become aroused, and attempt to force it up the spine and thus achieve enlightenment themselves. This is an orgasm in its purest form.

But what is an orgasm?

The best description of an orgasm can be found in a book by Wilhelm Reich called *The Function of the Orgasm*. First published in English in 1941, it details Reich's clinical research into what he called 'sex-economy.' Being a Freudian by trade, he believed anxiety and neuroses were a systematic result of the lack of a proper, fully functioning individual. This was particularly so during sex, and the inability to have a proper orgasm was due to 'genital anxiety,' or what we would call today 'hang ups.' He described an orgasm as 'a full paroxysm of the body.' To obviate any neurosis or anxiety the individual should experience this full paroxysm of the body on a regular basis. Reich calculated that on average an individual should experience at least 4000 of these during his lifetime. Only then would there be a guarantee that he is free of anxiety and other conflicts, and then go on to experience life as a fit, healthy, full-functioning individual. Reich believed that lack of orgasm was down to internal disorders and the blocking of energy. He would later expand this theory with his discovery of what he called 'orgone energy,' which is identical with *prana, ojas*, etc. If this energy is blocked in any way, then lack of orgasm is the result. Conversely, the maximum expenditure of this orgone energy leads to a full orgasm.

It is immaterial whether Reich's theory is correct or not, but I would say it is based on sound principles. If we take, for example, nature at its simplest, we can look at how nature works according to her own laws. If we view a stream, it naturally runs downhill, the water being forced by gravity to seek its own level. However, if we were to block the course of that stream by building a dam across it, the flow of water would be impeded and it would be unable to pursue its natural progression downhill. It would accumulate at the dam, build up and find another outlet, either by flowing eventually around the object or, if it builds up enough, over the object. This is exactly the same with natural energy in the body; if it becomes blocked through some internal agency, it would have to find another form of outlet, resulting in neurotic behaviour.

Continuing this analogy, if we could get this flow of energy to move properly, in accordance with its own laws, and harness it correctly, then we could channel it and help it flow to its greatest expression.

And that is exactly what my programme is all about; developing a means whereby we channel this subtle energy of the body, control it, and then force it towards its natural outlet (i.e. the genitals) with the accompanying result of an orgasm.

There is nothing tactual in my programme; there is no touching involved whatsoever. It is also non-penetrative sex without the nudity. The host of this show simply arouses *ojas* in himself, transmits it to his subject, focuses it in the genital region and brings it out through the genitals. It is as simple as that.

So, as the production companies for the major channels in the UK rejected this rather interesting idea in favour of bland rubbish like 'Big Brother,' 'X Factor,' 'Britain's Got Talent' (very questionable, in my opinion), etc., they are now going to pay for it. It's payback time. It is now also showtime. Enjoy.

Jon Lange
Summer 2014

PART ONE

TITLE: THE BIG O SHOW

PROD. No.: 319331

RUNNING TIME: Approx. 55 mins (inc. ads)

BROADCAST TIME: 22.00

BROADCAST DATE: 25/12/2015

Cue TITLE:

THE BIG O SHOW

Cue MUSIC:

Rimsky-Korsakov's *Scheherazade,* opening movement.

EXT. STUDIO. NIGHT.

CU: Notice on studio doors: 'STRICTLY ADULTS ONLY. NO TICKET, NO ENTRY. PATRONS ARE ADVISED THAT THIS SHOW ENCOURAGES AUDIENCE-PARTICIPATION. ANY PATRONS WHO HAVE SERIOUS HEART CONDITIONS ARE ADVISED NOT TO PARTICPATE. ALSO, SPARE UNDERWEAR IS ADVISABLE, IF NOT ESSENTIAL.'

The doors open. We go through the doors into the studio.

INT. STUDIO. NIGHT.

Cue APPLAUSE.
Lights UP:

We now focus on empty, flood-lit stage, and black curtains at back. Curtains open, HOST enters through curtains, and stands centre stage.

Cue more APPLAUSE.

HOST, dressed all in black, takes his applause with a bow and faces seated AUDIENCE with a big smile. He slowly raises his hands above his head, bringing them together, fingertips to fingertips, thumb to thumb.

CU: HOST'S hands, forming the letter 'O'.

Cue more APPLAUSE.

HOST brings down his hands, and bows to AUDIENCE again.

Cut MUSIC.

SILENCE.

HOST

Thank you, thank you. And welcome to a special show tonight. Each one of you is in for a real treat. And I can guarantee you will never have seen before anything like what we have in store tonight. Remember, this isn't about me, it's about you. And we want you to enjoy every minute of it, whether you're a young adult or an old one, whether you're rich or poor, married or single, we promise you, you will enjoy what we have lined up for you. So you are going to enjoy tonight, aren't you?

AUDIENCE: Yes!

HOST

Good. And I can see you are all eager to find out what this is all about.

You have been invited here for a little demonstration. And when you received your invitation you would've also had a reminder to bring some spare underwear with you tonight because, believe me, you will probably need it, especially those of you who tend to get more carried away than others, as we will soon find out.

But first, let me introduce myself. I am a yoga practitioner, or a yogi, as some prefer to call themselves, and I have been practising yoga for over twenty years. Now, most people, when we mention the word yoga they think of those strange positions and all those contortions that people put themselves in. That is only one form of yoga. Those positions, by the way, are called asanas, and they are especially designed to clear the subtle nerve channels of the body, allowing it to function properly. That is called Hatha Yoga. But there are other types of yoga not so familiar here in the West, like Raja Yoga, Kama Yoga, Bhakti Yoga, etc., all of which work with the body and the mind so that both reach equipoise and the body and mind become harmonious and in sync.

But there is another type of yoga, very little understood, especially in this country, and it is more akin to Tantra, which most of you have no doubt heard of. I stumbled across this other yoga many years ago when I was studying under my guru. He manipulated the subtle nerve channels in my body which he said had become blocked. And how he did it was rather remarkable because, although he used his hands, he didn't actually touch me. In fact, he didn't lay a finger on me, but made various passes over the vital centres of my body. And then I had this strange, but incredible, sensation, as if something was moving inside me, uncoiling like a spring and, I am ashamed to admit, I had a spontaneous ejaculation in his presence, something that hasn't happened to me since I hit puberty.

(AUDIENCE: Laughter, plus slight giggling.)

But he said, it was okay, that it was perfectly normal, and that it was a sign that the energy was now free. I was now unblocked, as he called it. Now this yoga of my old guru uses a type of energy known as ojas. This ojas is very subtle, so subtle in fact that you cannot see it, you cannot smell it, you cannot taste it, but you can feel it, especially when it courses through your body. It is used in practises like Ayurveda for healing, etc., and it is the essential energy of the body similar to what you could call the fluid of life. In man this ojas manifests physically as semen. In woman it is the vaginal secretions when she is aroused. In fact, that is the only time you will actually see it, or rather see its physical counterpart. And there's one critical moment when all of us adults can feel it more so than at any other time; that is when we are having an orgasm—the big O of this show.

So what we are going to do here tonight is to make all of you become aware of this ojas as you've never experienced it before, in a very intense way, and in a very concentrated form. By using my hands I am going to channel it, just as my old guru did for me, and bring it to the surface by producing an orgasm in each and every one of you. Few of you probably realise that an orgasm is actually a manifestation of this ojas but in its purest form.

Now, we all know what an orgasm is, don't we?

AUDIENCE: Yes (plus slight laughter).

HOST

Good. I thought you might. But is there anyone here who doesn't know what an orgasm really is?

AUDIENCE: (they all go quiet).

HOST

It's alright; there is no need to be shy here. We are all in this together, so let's loosen our inhibitions. Who enjoys a good orgasm?

AUDIENCE: (all raise their hands).

HOST

I thought so. But is there anybody here who hasn't had a good orgasm, or doesn't ever experience one?

Camera pans AUDIENCE'S faces. They remain quiet.

HOST

Now don't be shy, for it is a known fact that some people are incapable of having an orgasm for whatever reason, and that's why we are here tonight. So let me ask again: is there anyone here who has never had an orgasm?

Camera pans AUDIENCE'S faces. Now one or two here and there put their hands up.

HOST

Right, I thought so. Now, I am not going to be so personal as to ask you why, I don't really want to know that anyway, so what we will do later is try and help you have a proper orgasm. Don't worry, I am not going to come up there and give you one myself personally ...

(AUDIENCE: Laughter.)

... No. In fact, I am not even going to leave this spot on this stage. I am going to stand right here and you are going to feel this ojas flow through you. And when it flows through you then you will have an orgasm. That's right. You don't even have to leave your seats. Just make sure you've got some spare underwear in case any of you have an 'accident.'

AUDIENCE: Laughter.

HOST

Now, what do we mean by an orgasm? We all think we know, don't we? Because it is part of our maturation, our sexual awakening. We think we have an inkling based on personal experience. Well, there was once a guy called Wilhelm Reich who wrote about it. His book was called 'The

Function of the Orgasm,' a great title. In that book he described the orgasm as a 'total paroxysm of the body.' That is, every nerve, every fibre of your being should feel alive at the point of orgasm. And if you don't feel that sensation it means that the subtle energy–or what he called orgone energy–flowing through your body was blocked. It was his mission to help people unblock this energy so that it could flow more freely. He also believed that we had a right to feel this full paroxysm of the body.

AUDIENCE: Yes (cheering).

HOST

That's right! Because we all want to feel one, don't we? Because it's the only time when we can say we feel well and truly alive. But he also believed that the average person in his lifetime should have at least 4000 good, healthy orgasms to vitiate any unwanted psychological illness or neurosis. Now, that might sound excessive—after all he was a Freudian

(AUDIENCE: Laughter.)

—so perhaps we can forgive him for some slight exaggeration. However, I happen to agree with him on that point. We shouldn't have just a few orgasms throughout our whole lifetimes; we should have thousands, hell, millions of them.

AUDIENCE: Yes (cheering).

HOST

(excited, shouting, punching hand in air)

That's right, millions of them. We want to have one every day, every morning when we wake up, every night when we go to sleep, every time we have a bath or a shower, every time we use the toilet, every time we sit down, every time we stand up, every time we get on a bus, or ride our motorcycle, or drive our car. Every time we eat, every time we go for a walk, every time we fall in love, and every time we go to bed with that special person. Hell, I want today to be National Orgasm Day. I want every day to be a National Orgasm Day. And why not? We deserve it! We deserve some pleasure in our lives. So let's celebrate and have a good orgasm. Why? Because it feels good!

AUDIENCE: Yes (cheering).

HOST

That's right. We have a right to have an orgasm ....

(AUDIENCE: Yes!)

... And I am going to show you how it is possible to have a proper one. I promise you, each and every one of you, that by the time we're finished here tonight you will all have that pleasure. So let's get on with it. But first I need an assistant, if not two. Let's bring on the ladies who are going to help us tonight.

HOST steps to side to wave to curtains at back. They open.

CU: Two LADIES wearing skin-tight matching black catsuits and high heels. They come through curtains pushing steel table on wheels to centre of stage. They stop, hands on hips, big smiles, facing AUDIENCE.

AUDIENCE: Applause (the odd wolf-whistle).

HOST

Ladies and gentlemen, please welcome two very special ladies, Sylvia and Sandy.

AUDIENCE: Applause.

SYLVIA and SANDY take a bow. They are both gorgeous, in their mid-twenties, and are very fit-looking.

HOST

Now these two lovely ladies have been working with me for over two years. They have been on the road with me the world over, for we have taken this show everywhere. Haven't we, ladies?

SYLVIA and SANDY nod and smile.

HOST

And we have always had a good time, haven't we?

SYLVIA

Yes. We always have a good time when we are with you.

HOST

Oh, you are so kind. So who would like to be the first tonight? Sylvia? Sandy?

SANDY

I'll go first.

HOST

Okay, Sandy, if you insist.

(to AUDIENCE)

Give a big welcome to Sandy, ladies and gentlemen.

AUDIENCE: Applause.

HOST
(to LADIES)

Thank you, Sandy. And we will see you later, Sylvia.

(to AUDIENCE)

Let's have a big thank you for Sylvia as well.

AUDIENCE: Applause.

SYLVIA exits stage, waving to AUDIENCE.

CU: HOST adjusting table. It has black leather upholstery on top. HOST brings up headrest. He then takes SANDY'S hand.

HOST

Now, my dear, if you will just climb aboard.

CU: SANDY getting on table, lying down, face up, her hands by her sides, smiling at HOST.

HOST

That's it, my dear, just lie back and relax.

(to AUDIENCE)

Now, ladies and gentlemen, Sandy is just going to lie there. And in a minute I will get her nice and relaxed. I'm not going to hypnotise her, but put her in a very light trance. And then what I'll do, just by using my hands, I will raise up some ojas to bring her to orgasm, and then you will see for yourself how it works.

CU: HOST rubbing his hands together, then spreading them palm-down over SANDY'S face—not touching it. Her eyes close, her body goes limp.

HOST

Now, all I'm doing is putting her into a light trance. I repeat, this is not hypnosis, just a very mild form of relaxation. To have a proper orgasm you need to be relaxed so that the energy can flow through you freely without hindrance. That's what Reich believed. So we are just getting her nice and relaxed. She is still conscious. She can hear every word I'm saying. All I'm doing is passing my hands over her face ...

(CU: HOST'S hands passing over SANDY'S face in small semi-circles.)

… so she can now feel the ojas flowing through my hands into her body, relieving any aches and pains. That's good. Just like that.

CU: HOST stops movement of hands and brings them up palm forward to show AUDIENCE.

HOST

See, there's nothing on my hands. They are empty. There is no trickery involved. And Sandy is now nicely relaxed.

CU: SANDY'S face. Her eyes are closed, a glimmer of a smile on her face.

HOST

Good. That is just how I want her. Now what I am going to do is to get ojas really flowing through my hands, but I need to conjure up the requisite amount first so it is concentrated in my hands, and then I will transmit this current of energy to Sandy. So, here we go.

CU: HOST rubbing his hands together hard.

HOST

As I rub my hands together like this I can feel a tingling sensation, especially in the fingertips. It's like they have got electricity passing through them. The palms of my hands are now starting to feel warm, very warm; in fact they are already getting hot, which indicates that the ojas is just right. So now what I am going to do is to transmit this energy to Sandy and that will stir up the ojas in her body, and then I will channel it towards her solar plexus area. So here we go. Watch this.

HOST steps towards table and lays his hands out flat, palm downwards. Starting with SANDY'S hands and arms, he works his hands up to her shoulders in large circles just above her skin.

CU: HOST'S hands, not touching SANDY, but about an inch above her skin.

CU: HOST'S face, the concentration on his face, his eyes almost half-closed.

HOST

I can now feel the ojas flowing through me into Sandy's body. As we move down towards her chest, notice her breasts. Notice how the nipples are already becoming hard.

CU: SANDY'S breasts, her nipples erect, almost poking through the thin black fabric of her catsuit.

HOST

As you can see, she is not wearing a bra.

CU: AUDIENCE'S faces as they have a good look at the monitors showing CU of SANDY. Some of them are smiling and obviously enjoying the view.

HOST

And now I am going to work this energy down towards her abdomen ...

(CU: HOST'S hands skimming over surface of SANDY'S chest and abdomen in large circles.)

.... like that and down to her pelvis. I'm going to stop there and now work on her feet, and bring this energy up her legs.

The HOST now stands by SANDY'S feet and starts manipulating his hands above her feet, in large circles, then up her legs, towards her pelvis. As he does so, we hear SANDY let out a light murmur.

CU: SANDY'S face. Her mouth is opening and closing, her eyes are in REM. She lets out a moan.

HOST

It is now beginning to work its magic. What I am doing here is draining all the energy in her extremities so it is concentrated in one area, namely her genitals. There is said to be at the base of the spine a sleeping serpent. So what I am doing now is getting it to wake up, arousing it out of its slumber, raising it up, and getting it to move towards her genitals.

As he does so, we can see SANDY'S body start to rock back and forth, her hands now gripping edge of table, her knuckles turning white.

CU: HOST'S hands working over genital area.

CU: SANDY'S face. It is now grimacing and her mouth emits an occasional moan.

CU: On AUDIENCE, their faces as they watch, fascinated.

HOST

I can feel it as I move my hands round this area. The ojas is coaxing the serpent out of its slumber and is now concentrated in her genitals.

CU: SANDY'S body is now rocking back and forth in time to the movement of HOST'S hands as if they are attached by invisible strings. When he passes his hands to the right hip, her right hip lifts. Then to her left hip, and her left hip lifts.

HOST

Now I am really going to get it working. My hands are hot, very hot with all this accumulated energy. I can feel them burning as I move in tighter circles around her vagina. And if I lift up my hands so does her whole pelvic area.

CU: SANDY'S body lifting in rhythm with HOST'S hands.

HOST is spreading his palms over SANDY'S genital area, in tighter circles, her whole body practically lifting off the table, her moaning becoming distinctly louder, her movements more ferocious and wilder as he moves his hands in ever tighter.

CU: HOST'S hands over SANDY, her body arching, lifting up and down with strong pelvic thrusts.

CU: HOST'S face, beads of sweat running down it.

CU: SANDY'S face, wild grimaces, her lips petulant, her mouth emitting strange noises, her eyes opening and closing, rolling up, going wild. Occasionally we see just the whites of her eyes.

SANDY, now in the height of passion, looks like she has become possessed with her body bouncing up and down on table, her legs kicking, her body arching, then collapsing, her hands gripping edge of table, trying to hold on to it.

CU: HOST'S hands over SANDY'S genitals. We can almost see through the thin fabric a damp patch is appearing.

Suddenly HOST stops.

SANDY'S body collapses on table in a heap, spent. It lies there inert as if drained of all energy and life.

CU: SANDY'S face, a big smile, her face flushed, her eyes all watery.

CU: HOST blowing air onto his hands.

HOST

Sorry, ladies and gentlemen, I just had to stop there. My hands are now burning hot.

(to side of STAGE)

Could I have some ice cold water, please?

Enter SYLVIA carrying towel and ice bucket on silver tray. She smiles at

HOST as she stops in front of him. He dips his hands in ice bucket.

CU: HOST'S hands in ice bucket, dipping in iced-water, steam coming off his hands.

HOST withdraws his hands, shakes them. SYLVIA hands towel to HOST who dries his hands.

HOST

(to SYLVIA as he hands back towel)

Thank you.

SYLVIA takes towel and exits with ice bucket and tray.

AUDIENCE: Applause.

HOST

(to AUDIENCE)

Thank you, thank you. You're so kind.

(to SANDY)

And how was it for you?

CU: HOST taking SANDY'S hand.

SANDY gets off table and bows to AUDIENCE.

AUDIENCE: Applause (more wolf-whistles).

SANDY is looking flushed, her cheeks practically aglow, smiling.

SANDY

That was wonderful; truly wonderful.

HOST

I am sorry I had to stop there. My hands were practically burning up.

SANDY

Boy, I'm sure glad you did. Otherwise I would have died.

HOST

It was that good?

SANDY

Hmmm, it was that good!

HOST
(to AUDIENCE)

Okay, well thank you, Sandy. Ladies and gentlemen, please give a big thank you to Sandy for being such a great sport tonight.

AUDIENCE: Applause.

SANDY bows once more and exits, waving to AUDIENCE.

HOST
(to SANDY)

That's right, love. You go and recover.

(to CAMERA)

And I am just going to have a short break myself to get back to normal. See you shortly.

HOST exits stage.

AUDIENCE: Applause.

FADE OUT.

Cue ADS.

PART TWO

FADE UP:

INT. STUDIO. NIGHT.

AUDIENCE: Applause.

HOST enters stage and stands centre stage, facing AUDIENCE.

HOST

Thank you, thank you. Just before the break we saw Sandy having an orgasm. I used my hands to manipulate the flow of ojas in her body and concentrated it in her sex-centre. She was truly satisfied afterwards. And didn't she look radiant?

AUDIENCE: Yes.

HOST

And there was no trickery involved. What she experienced was real; it wasn't fake. It wasn't put on just for show. She had a genuine orgasm without physical contact. So you're probably now thinking it was just her; that somehow she is highly susceptible to my influence. Well, I don't want you to think that at all. And I am going to prove it by now carrying out the same procedure with Sylvia. So, ladies and gentleman, let's give a big warm welcome for Sylvia again.

AUDIENCE: Applause (some wolf-whistles).

Enter SYLVIA from back stage, through curtains, bowing to AUDIENCE and waving.

CU: SYLVIA, a big smile on her face.

SYLVIA stands next to HOST, centre stage. He gives her a quick peck on the cheek.

HOST

Hello, Sylvia. And how are you feeling tonight?

SYLVIA

Oh, I'm feeling great.

HOST

You'll be feeling even better in a minute. Now, let's just clear this up for the audience and the viewers at home. How many times have we done this show?

SYLVIA

Oh, I can't remember exactly, but I would say loads of times.

HOST

Yes, loads, many, many times. And did you ever fake your orgasm when I brought you to the point of climax?

SYLVIA

No, never.

HOST

So each time was genuine?

SYLVIA

Indeed. Absolutely.

HOST

Good. So what we are going to do now is do the same as I did with Sandy, and give you a full body paroxysm. So, if you will just take up your position.

CU: HOST holding SYLVIA'S hand as he escorts her to table.

SYLVIA gets on table and lies down, face up, hands by her side.

HOST

That's right, just lie back. Relax.

(to AUDIENCE)

We're going to do exactly the same thing as we did with Sandy. Again there will be no trickery involved, and again I'm not going to touch her, but simply apply ojas through the laying on of hands. First, I need to get the energy flowing. So again I'm simply going to rub my hands together.

CU: HOST'S hands, rubbing them together.

HOST

I can already feel it flowing into my hands. They are getting warmer, and the circulation is increasing. I am now going to put Sylvia into a very light trance, and get her nice and relaxed.

CU: HOST'S hands over SYLVIA'S face, working in tight circles, her eyes closing, face becoming relaxed.

HOST

That's it, perfect. Now she is in a trance. You can see already her whole body going limp.

CU: SYLVIA'S body. We pan from head to feet, the body limp, hands fallen by her side.

HOST

And now I am going to start working with the ojas, get it flowing through her body, starting with the hands and arms first. So what we are doing here is moving it away from her extremities and concentrating it around her solar plexus.

CU: HOST'S hands, working in tight circles around her hands, up her arms to her shoulders, then down to the centre of her body.

HOST

And the same thing again. We can already see a visible difference. Her nipples are getting hard.

CU: SYLVIA'S breasts, her nipples practically poking through the thin black fabric of her catsuit; no bra visible.

HOST

And now I'm going to work from her other end, starting at her feet and moving up her legs.

HOST stands at end of table, his hands working over SYLVIA'S feet, then up her legs, towards her pelvis. As we reach this, we see a slight tremor roll up her legs towards her pelvis. The whole area moves. SYLVIA lets out a moan.

CU: SYLVIA'S face, her mouth, her lips. She is practically biting them. Her eyes roll up with the eyelids flickering.

CU: HOST'S hands working in tight circles over SYLVIA'S crutch, her legs opening and closing in time to his movements.

We can hear moans escaping from SYLVIA'S mouth, and see her body arching, her hands gripping edge of table, trying to hold on.

We now see HOST working harder, bringing SYLVIA to complete orgasm, her body writhing in ecstasy like she's got a pneumatic drill up her, pumping away hard.

SYLVIA lets out a scream.

CU: SYLVIA'S face, it is contorting, flushed with blood, her eyes closed like tight creases, her teeth biting her lips.

CU: HOST'S face, sweating profusely, his eyes half-closed as if in a trance himself.

CU: SYLVIA'S body thumping on table as she lifts up and down, her knuckles white, her crutch damp.

CU: AUDIENCE'S faces, staring at spectacle, some with mouths agape.

As HOST pushes SYLVIA beyond the point of ecstasy, her body starts thudding on table harder, making loud sounds as her backside hits leather upholstery of table. Then suddenly he stops, backs off. SYLVIA lets out sigh of relief. Her body goes limp, hands falling by side, looking dead.

AUDIENCE: Applause (some give standing ovation and wolf whistles).

CU: HOST bowing to AUDIENCE showing his hands are red hot. He now blows on them.

CU: SYLVIA, regaining some composure, opens her eyes, tears of joy running down her cheeks.

HOST

Thank you, thank you. Wow! Wasn't that great!

AUDIENCE: Yes (cheering).

HOST
(to SIDE)

Can I have some more water, please?

Enter SANDY, wearing a new catsuit, this time white, carrying towel and ice bucket on silver tray. She stops in front of HOST. He dips his hands in bucket of iced-water, steam coming off them, and then dries them on towel handed to him by SANDY.

HOST
(to SANDY)

Thank you.

HOST hands towel back to SANDY. She takes it, backs off with tray, exits, waving to AUDIENCE.

AUDIENCE: Applause.

HOST
(to AUDIENCE)

I don't know about you but I feel like I've just had ten thousand volts pass through me.

(to SYLVIA)

And how about you, Sylvia?

CU: HOST taking SYLVIA'S hand, helping her off table.

SYLVIA stands next to HOST looking like she is going to collapse any minute, barely able to stand properly, wobbling, legs buckling slightly, gripping HOST'S hand to help stay upright and not fall over.

SYLVIA

Oh, I have definitely had ten thousand volts up me. Phew!

AUDIENCE: Laughter.

HOST

It looks like it. So, tell you what, you go and recover whilst we take another quick break.

(to CAMERA)

See you shortly.

AUDIENCE: Applause.

FADE OUT.

Cue ADS.

PART THREE

FADE UP:

INT. STUDIO. NIGHT.

HOST enters from back stage through curtains, stands centre stage.

AUDIENCE: Applause.

HOST

Thank you, thank you. Just before the break we saw Sylvia experience an orgasm, probably about the best she's ever had. It looked at one point like she was going to explode. Now, I know what you may be thinking; she was faking it. So to prove that she wasn't, what we are going to do now is ask for a volunteer from the audience.

HOST stands still surveying AUDIENCE. They have all gone quiet and are looking at each other nervously.

HOST

Now don't be shy. Come on. Isn't anyone going to volunteer? No? Come on, let's have someone. I am not going to hurt you. Don't be embarrassed. A lady? A gentleman? Anyone? I'm not fussy, or so my wife keeps telling me.

AUDIENCE: Laughter.

CU: AUDIENCE'S faces, some laughing, some nervous.

Not one person puts their hand up. We can hear whispering in the AUDIENCE.

HOST

Please, let's have someone; otherwise everyone will think we're faking this. So the only way we can prove we're not faking it is by having someone step down from the audience and then we'll prove it. This could be the best orgasm you're ever going to turn down. Look at it this way; it may even help your sex-life.

Suddenly a LADY in the AUDIENCE puts her hand up.

CU: LADY with hand up.

HOST

Thank you. Give a round of applause to our volunteer.

AUDIENCE: Applause.

HOST

Come on down, love.

CU: HOST gesticulating for LADY to come down, and clapping.

LADY leaves her seat and steps towards stage, enters stage, looking nervous.

AUDIENCE: Applause.

HOST

That's it. Now don't be shy. Come on, there's nothing to be embarrassed about. We're all adults here.

LADY stands next to HOST facing AUDIENCE.

AUDIENCE: Applause stops, now very quiet.

HOST

Thank you. Just stand there, my dear. That's right. Let's have a good look at you. You're a fine looking woman. What's you name?

LADY

Jane.

HOST

And where are you from, Jane?

JANE

I'm from Croydon.

AUDIENCE: Slight applause and cheering.

HOST

Oh, it sounds like you brought some fans with you. Now, did you also bring some spare underwear with you as well?

(JANE: Nodding.)

Good, because you may need them. Now, how old are you, Jane?

JANE

I'm 27.

HOST

A good age. And are you married, engaged or single?

JANE

I've got a boyfriend.

HOST

Oh, good. And is he here with you tonight?

JANE

He is indeed. That's him over there.

JANE points to the GENTLEMAN she was sitting next to.

HOST

And what's his name?

JANE

Colin.

HOST
(to COLIN)

Hello, Colin.

CU: COLIN smiling, waving back to HOST.

HOST

You don't mind if I just borrow your girlfriend for a few minutes, do you?

AUDIENCE: Laughter.

CU: COLIN smiling, shaking his head.

HOST
(to JANE)

Good. Now, Jane, let's get this straight for the other members of the audience, and for the viewers at home; we have never met before, have we?

(JANE: Shaking her head.)

And this is the first time we have actually met, isn't it?

(JANE: Nodding her head.)

And as far as you know, you are in good health and there's nothing physically wrong with you?

JANE

That's correct.

HOST

And how long have you been going out with Colin?

JANE

Over two years now.

HOST

And do you have any children?

JANE

No, not yet.

HOST

And would you like some? I'm mean not now, but in the future?

AUDIENCE: Laughter.

JANE

Yes, maybe next year.

HOST

Well, let's hope you have many. Don't worry, I'm not going to get too personal. I just want to make sure that everything is okay.

JANE

Everything is fine.

HOST

Good. Now, all I want you to do is lie on the table, relax, and forget who you are and where you are. Just allow your body to speak its own language, okay? By that I mean, give in to your body. Don't fight against the urges you may be feeling. Allow them to come to the surface. It's a bit like therapy where you just shut off your mind and go with the flow, as they say.

AUDIENCE: Laughter.

HOST takes JANE'S hand and walks her to table.

HOST
(to SIDE)

If I could have my two assistants back, please.

Enter SANDY and SYLVIA from backstage. SYLVIA is also wearing a new catsuit, also in white.

AUDIENCE: Applause (some wolf-whistling).

SANDY and SYLVIA take JANE'S hands and help her climb on to table. JANE lies back and relaxes. SANDY and SYLVIA pat JANE on the shoulder for good luck and step back out of HOST'S way.

HOST
(to AUDIENCE)

Now, I want you to know that I have never done it with Jane before. And this will be the first time she's had an orgasm in public, or at least I think it will be her first time ...

(AUDIENCE: Laughter.)

.... And I have every confidence that she will enjoy what she is about to experience. So, I'm going to do the same thing I did with Sandy and Sylvia. I am going to put Jane into a very light trance. First, I want to get the ojas flowing like this ....

(CU: HOST rubbing his hands together.)

... and now I am going to apply it to Jane.

HOST goes over to JANE. He starts making semi-circles above her head with his hands, palms down. Already JANE is closing her eyes.

CU: JANE'S eyes, they are closing.

HOST

She is now in a light trance. So I am going to do exactly as I did before. I am going to bring the ojas up from her extremities, up her arms and down her shoulders to her solar plexus.

CU: HOST working his hands over JANE'S arms, shoulders and down her body to her abdomen. As we pan down we can see her nipples are erect, poking through her dress, even though she is wearing a bra.

HOST

And I'm now going to the other end.

HOST moves to JANE'S feet. He starts working small circles over her feet, up her legs towards her pelvic area.

CU: HOST'S hands, working up her legs.

CU: JANE'S hands gripping edge of table, knuckles turning white.

CU: JANE'S face, her eyes in REM, her lips quivering, her mouth opening and closing, emitting the odd moan.

CU: AUDIENCE'S faces staring at CU on monitors, fascinated.

CU: COLIN'S face, intrigued.

HOST

And now I am going to do the same. I am going to awaken the sleeping serpent, get it out of its slumber.

CU: HOST'S hands working tight circles over JANE'S crutch.

Suddenly her body, which was limp, jumps up about an inch off table, and very visibly something is stirring deep inside her. We can hear her moan. We see the odd spasmodic movement in her pelvis.

HOST is now working over crutch area; as he moves his hands over JANE'S body, her body seems to follow. Then he moves them in a large circle around her pelvis, and her hips sway with each movement. Her hands grip edge of table tighter and tighter, her body starts thudding against upholstery, her moans getting louder. We can hear the dull thudding sound as her backside starts hitting table repeatedly.

CU: HOST'S face, the concentration in his eyes, beads of sweat breaking out all over his face.

CU: HOST'S hands, just above JANE'S crutch, now working in tight circles, bringing all the energy to her vagina. We see, through her dress, that she is now wet.

HOST and JANE seem to be working in tandem; when he raises his hands over her body, her body appears to move, lifting up off table. We hear JANE emit a loud scream.

Suddenly HOST stops and pulls back. JANE goes silent, limp. HOST stands to face AUDIENCE.

AUDIENCE: Applause.

HOST bows to AUDIENCE. SANDY and SYLVIA step forward. SYLVIA exits stage, returns with towel and ice bucket on tray. HOST dips hands in iced-water. SANDY mops his brow with towel, helps him wipe his hands. SYLVIA exits with towel and ice bucket on tray. She returns and stands next to HOST with SANDY.

HOST

Thank you, thank you. You're so kind. Wow! I really thought I was going to die for a minute then.

(to JANE)

And what about you, Jane?

CU: JANE'S face, her eyes opening, all watery, her cheeks all flushed, her make-up slightly smudged.

SANDY and SYLVIA help JANE to sit up and get off table. As JANE steps off table, and puts her foot on floor, her leg buckles and she begins to fall. SANDY and SYLVIA catch JANE, preventing her from falling to floor. They help her to stand straight.

AUDIENCE: Laughter.

CU: HOST'S face, smirking, trying not to laugh.

CU: JANE'S face, looking embarrassed as if she has badly wet herself.

SANDY and SYLVIA take JANE to HOST. She stands next to him, centre stage and faces AUDIENCE.

JANE

Sorry.

HOST

Don't apologise. You've just had one of the best experiences of your life.

(to AUDIENCE)

Doesn't she look great?

AUDIENCE: Yes!

CU: JANE looking radiant.

CU: HOST applauding JANE.

HOST
(to JANE)

Well that was good for me. By the looks of it, it was obviously good for you too....

(JANE: Light laugh.)

... and hopefully you will have many more like that to come in the future. I think you better go and sit down next to your boyfriend and recover. Ladies and gentlemen, give a big thank you to Jane for being such a wonderful sport.

HOST, SANDY and SYLVIA start clapping as JANE exits stage.

AUDIENCE: Applause.

HOST

Wow, that was really great. I could feel the energy flowing through me like I had just turned on a tap. And I can still feel it flowing through me, so why not have another volunteer? Come on. Come on. Let's have someone else from the audience. Preferably a man this time. Now, who's going to volunteer?

Camera pans AUDIENCE. One or two men put a hand up nervously.

HOST

Good, that's what I want. A man this time, just to prove I can do it with both sexes. How about you, sir?

HOST points to GENT on right of AUDIENCE with his hand up.

CU: GENT'S face, smiling.

HOST

Yes you, sir. How would you like to have the best time of your life?

CU: GENT'S face, nodding.

HOST

Good, then come on down.

HOST starts clapping.

AUDIENCE: Applause.

The GENT leaves his seat and enters stage, standing next to HOST. GENT faces AUDIENCE.

HOST
(to GENT)

And what's your name?

GENT

Adam.

HOST

Okay, Adam. And where are you from?

ADAM

I am originally from South Africa, but I now live in Surbiton.

HOST

I thought I noticed a slight accent there. And what do you do for a living, Adam?

ADAM

I sell marketing products for a major firm.

HOST

Good. And I take it you're very successful in your job?

ADAM

Reasonably proficient, yes.

HOST

That's excellent. Well, Adam, just to confirm with the audience and the viewers at home, we haven't met before, have we?

ADAM

Never.

HOST

And this is the first time you've been to one of my shows?

ADAM

That's correct.

HOST

Now, I can see you're married. Have you brought your wife with you?

ADAM

I have indeed. She's sitting up there.

ADAM points to LADY in AUDIENCE.

CU: LADY'S face, smiling.

HOST

And what's her name?

ADAM

It's Jacqueline, but she prefers to be called Jackie.

HOST
(to JACKIE)

Hi, Jackie. I'm about to give your husband the best experience he's ever going to have. That's not meant to be a slur on your part ....

(AUDIENCE: Laughter.)

... and hopefully he can pass it on to you afterwards.

AUDIENCE: More laughter.

(to ADAM)

And do you have any kids?

ADAM

We do. A boy and a girl

HOST

Good. And what are their names and ages?

ADAM

Well, Michael is now coming up for 4, and Gina is 2.

HOST

That's lovely. And are you planning on having any more?

ADAM

We will do if we can get a bigger house. At the moment we only have two bedrooms.

HOST

Well, good luck. So we have established that everything is okay, and that you have no marital problems. But what about your health?

ADAM

Fine. I had a check up the other week.

HOST

That's wonderful. So what I am going to do with you, Adam, is exactly the same as I did with Sandy, Sylvia and Jane over there, who's still recovering.

AUDIENCE: Laughter.

CU: JANE'S face, blushing.

HOST gesticulates to SYLVIA and SANDY to take ADAM to table. They help him on to it. ADAM lies back and relaxes. SYLVIA and SANDY step back out of HOST'S way.

HOST

Good, that's perfect. Now it may seem a bit different because I am a man about to give another man an orgasm, but really there is no difference as we all have the same amount of ojas, regardless of sex. I am going to apply the same technique that I used on the ladies. The only difference, I would say here, is that it may take a bit longer. Some men tend to take longer to get aroused. But a woman can become aroused very quickly. She can also have multiple orgasms and ride on the crest of a wave for a long time, whereas a man can only have one orgasm at a time, and then he is spent. The obvious indication tonight will be seeing Adam have an ejaculation. So let's hope he has been sensible and brought some spare pants with him tonight ....

(AUDIENCE: Laughter.)

... But sometimes a man doesn't always experience an orgasm when he ejaculates. Sometimes it is completely absent. So with Adam I am going to make sure he has a full body paroxysm. And hopefully this will be one of many he will experience, especially with his wife. Because what he should be able to do after tonight is pass the experience on to his sexual partner, and she in turn will have the same proportionate amount of full body paroxysm. So, let's see how it goes. As I said, it may take a bit longer, and it may take a bit more effort. But it's going to be worth it, I can assure you.

CU: HOST rubbing his hands together.

HOST moves over to table and places his hands palm down just over ADAM'S face.

CU: HOST'S hands over ADAM'S face, his eyes slowly closing.

HOST

So what I am doing now is exactly the same as with the others; I'm putting Adam into a very light trance, just helping him to get nice and relaxed. It's very important for a man to be relaxed when he is about to come for if he isn't relaxed he may suffer from premature ejaculation, or he may not be able to give in to his body and let it speak its own language. Remember, it's the man who has to get the erection, not the woman, and for that reason sometimes it is tougher on the man, but sometimes you find it's also easier to get him aroused.

So, I've put Adam into a light trance. What I'm going to do now is get more ojas flowing through my hands, so I'm going to rub them for a bit.

CU: HOST rubbing hands together.

HOST

Now I can already feel my hands warming up. They are getting really warm, so that means they are ready.

HOST steps over to ADAM. He now places his hands above ADAM'S hands and arms, working them in tight circles just above his body. Then on to the shoulders and down his body to the solar plexus.

CU: ADAM'S face, his eyelids flickering, now in REM, a slight smile of pleasure on his lips.

CU: ADAM'S chest. We can see too his nipples are becoming erect through his white shirt.

HOST moves down to other end, bending over ADAM'S feet. He passes his hands over the feet, and starts moving them up his legs.

When he reaches ADAM'S crotch we can see a visible bulge in his trousers.

CU: ADAM'S crotch, slight bulge in trousers.

CU: AUDIENCE'S faces staring at CU on monitors, some of them sniggering. LADIES in AUDIENCE going 'Wow.'

HOST

Now I am going to get the serpent awake and bring him to this area here.

CU: HOST'S hands over crotch, moving in tight circles.

CU: ADAM'S hands gripping edge of table.

CU: ADAM'S crotch, big bulge in trousers.

We can hear ADAM moaning and see his body jerking around the waist as HOST moves in tight circles over crotch area.

We can see ADAM is now truly erect, his body hopping, his pelvis thrusting, more moans escaping from his lips. It looks like he is going to explode any minute.

CU: ADAM'S face now all red with excitement, his eyes open, rolling wildly as the force takes control of him.

CU: HOST'S face, concentration in his eyes, beads of sweat rolling down his cheeks.

HOST works ever tighter circles over ADAM'S crotch, concentrating on his penis. Suddenly ADAM'S feet are kicking wildly, his head is tossing all over the place, his pelvis thrusting up and down, then his whole body goes stiff. ADAM ejaculates. He lets out a dying scream as his body goes limp on table.

CU: ADAM'S crotch, a visible sign of his ejaculation; it's all wet.

CU: ADAM'S face, looking like he's been through hell, water running out of his eyes and down his face.

HOST stops, steps back, raising his hands in the air. SYLVIA exits stage, returns with towel and ice bucket on tray. SANDY steps forward with towel from SYLVIA to mop HOST'S brow. SYLVIA presents bucket. HOST dips his hands in bucket. He cools down his hands, steam coming off them. He dries his hands with towel and returns it to SANDY. SYLVIA and SANDY exit stage with towel and ice bucket on tray. HOST takes a bow.

AUDIENCE: Applause (some giving standing ovation).

HOST

Thank you, thank you. You're very kind. Wow! That was amazing. That man just didn't want to come. I thought we were going to be here all night. I've never had to work so hard in my life.

AUDIENCE: Laughter.

SYLVIA and SANDY enter stage. They help ADAM to get off table. He struggles to his feet, knees practically buckling, and face all flushed.

HOST
(to ADAM)

Can you walk?

AUDIENCE: Laughter.

SYLVIA and SANDY help ADAM stand next to HOST, facing AUDIENCE.

HOST
(to ADAM)

I don't need to ask, as it is written all over your face, but obviously you enjoyed that.

ADAM

Wow, that was amazing. Unbelievable!

HOST

Good.

(to AUDIENCE)

Ladies and gentlemen, please give a big hand to Adam here who has been an excellent participant.

AUDIENCE: Applause.

ADAM exits stage, helped by SYLVIA and SANDY.

HOST
(to CAMERA)

Now we are going to take another quick break, and when we come back we are going to finish off tonight with the big finale. See you shortly.

AUDIENCE: Applause.

FADE OUT.

Cue ADS.

PART FOUR

FADE UP:

INT. STUDIO. NIGHT.

AUDIENCE: Applause.

Camera pans AUDIENCE. HOST enters stage and stands centre stage.

CU: HOST bowing to AUDIENCE.

HOST

Welcome back. That's nearly it, folks. It's been a very tiring night for myself, but I'm sure you have enjoyed it, and hopefully you now all believe that ojas actually exists. What I would love to do is get everyone of you up on this table tonight and give everyone of you the same treatment that I have given Sylvia, Sandy, Jane and now Adam. But unfortunately that is not possible, time is running out, and it would probably kill me ....

(AUDIENCE: Laughter.)

... and I don't want to die just yet. So what I am going to do now is to try and get ojas flowing through all of you simultaneously. That's right; you're all going to have one big orgasm together ...

(AUDIENCE: Laughter, some nervous.)

... but you have to be in the mood. So I want you all to relax, just sit back in your seat and I want you all to hold hands with the person sitting next to you.

CU: AUDIENCE holding hands.

HOST

That's right. I don't care if it's not your partner or a complete stranger, because we're all in this together. So what I am going to do, I am going to start on this side of the audience ...

(*HOST points to left.*)

... and I am going to work my way across, so it will be like a wave rolling over all of you as I project ojas at you and you will find it hitting you gently. Let it flow through you. Don't hold it back, just ride with it. I want you all to open up, forget who you are, and just go with the flow.

This is going to be one hell of an experiment, so here it goes.

HOST steps to the left side of stage and starts rubbing his hands together.

HOST

I am now going to project ojas at this side first, and then this is going to move all the way across and as it hits each one of you, you will feel relaxed, alert, but not sleepy.

HOST projects ojas by flinging his arms forwards to members of AUDIENCE on left-hand side. They start to look relaxed. Then he projects ojas to the middle, and then to the right. All of AUDIENCE is looking very relaxed.

CU: AUDIENCE'S faces, relaxed.

CU: HOST rubbing his hands together again.

HOST now starts working up some power by swaying his arms around and then directing it to the left side of AUDIENCE. He repeats this three times, throwing his whole self into the act. As he does so, some of the AUDIENCE look like they have just been hit by a tidal wave from the left.

CU: AUDIENCE'S faces, the men looking startled as if something is happening inside them. Then they look down at their laps. Some of them are embarrassed. The women too look startled, feeling the ojas flowing through them. A few give out moans as wave after wave hits them. They too look embarrassed and look down at their laps, their jaws dropping.

CU: AUDIENCE'S hands, clasping each other tightly.

The camera pans left to right, AUDIENCE in ecstasy, some moaning loudly.

HOST steps back on to stage, letting the power drop.

AUDIENCE looks flushed as if they have all had an orgasm, and a very pleasurable experience as they come out of the light trance and unclasp hands, some of them looking nervously at their laps, some giggling.

AUDIENCE: Applause.

HOST

Thank you, thank you. Well I hope you all enjoyed that. I did, and I could really feel it flowing through me to you. As I was doing it I was watching all your faces light up one by one ....

(AUDIENCE: Laughter.)

... Honestly, it was like someone had just turned on the illuminations at Blackpool ....

(AUDIENCE: Laughter.)

... Well, that's it. Now you know what it feels like to have ojas flowing through you. All you have to do is relax and let go. Don't fight against the natural urges of your body, give into them, and you'll be far more satisfied thereby.

But I am not satisfied! You've all had an orgasm. Sylvia and Sandy have had an orgasm. Even Jane and Adam have had an orgasm. But I haven't. And I think it's only fair that we should end tonight's show with me having a little orgasm of my own. Don't you think?

AUDIENCE: Yes.

HOST turns to side of stage.

HOST

Can I have my apparatus and cape, please?

Enter SYLVIA and SANDY carrying HOST'S cape and apparatus. SYLVIA hands apparatus to HOST.

HOST
(to SYLVIA and SANDY)

Thank you, my dears.

(to AUDIENCE)

Now, in case you are wondering what on earth this is, it's my apparatus that by law I have to use when performing in public. It's not just to protect the prudish, but also, as everyone knows, it is illegal to show a bare erect penis on national TV. So for decency's sake what I am going to do is strap this belt round my waist ...

(CU: HOST strapping belt round waist with a loose leather strap just below crotch.)

... there you go, just like that. And if I could have my jar ...

(*SYLVIA hands HOST jar. HOST holds jar aloft.*)

... As you can see it is empty. But we will soon fix that ....

(CU: HOST strapping empty jar next to his crotch.)

... And if I could have my cape, please....

(*SANDY hands HOST his cape.*)

... Now, by law I have to wear this because I have to cover the offending part like this ....

(CU: HOST putting on cape, covering his front so jar is no longer visible.)

....And if I just get out my manhood ...

(*We hear HOST unzip his flies and see him fumbling under cape.*)

... And rest it in the jar like that ...

(*HOST'S hands come up from under cape.*)

(CU: On jar, hidden under cape.)

... I assure you there's no trickery involved here. As I have said, I have to do this by law otherwise this show will never get aired. But don't you just hate it when you can't see what's going on, like those magicians on stage who cannot perform their illusions without doing it behind a screen or a curtain? Well, there's no trick here. This is for real, and without hands. Watch.

HOST stands still, waves his hands in the air to show they are empty, and then raises them above his head in the shape of the letter 'O' and brings them together, rubbing them gently, and then lowers them down the front. As he does so, his eyes close. He moves his hands round and round in tight circles by his crotch, but not touching it.

CU: On HOST'S crotch and noticeable slight erection under cape.

CU: On HOST'S face, his eyes closed in ecstasy, his lips trembling.

HOST starts to sway to and fro, his pelvis thrusting slightly forward, as SANDY and SLVIA look on either side of HOST.

HOST'S hands go up as he makes sudden spasmodic movement.

CU: HOST'S crotch, penis twitching under cape and then going limp.

CU: HOST'S face, looking flushed but now relieved.

HOST brings his hands down. They disappear under cape and we see movement underneath. HOST pulls out jar and holds it aloft to show AUDIENCE.

CU: On HOST'S jar; there is now sperm in it.

AUDIENCE: Applause.

HOST hands jar to SYLVIA. She takes it and exits stage. HOST'S hands disappear under cape and we hear his flies being zipped up and see him adjust himself. He removes cape, handing it to SANDY. He removes his apparatus, handing it also to SANDY. SANDY exits. HOST faces AUDIENCE and bows.

AUDIENCE: Applause.

HOST bows again, and then gesticulates to side of stage. SYLVIA and SANDY enter stage, join him either side, take his hands and bow with him to AUDIENCE.

HOST

Thank you, thank you. You have been a smashing audience tonight. And we hope all your orgasms in the future will be great, if not fantastic ones. Thanks to all of you again for being such great sports. Get home safely, and maybe we will see all of you again the next time we are here. So from Sylvia, Sandy and me, it's goodnight.

HOST, SYLVIA and SANDY bow once more to AUDIENCE and exit stage, waving to AUDIENCE.

FADE OUT.

Cue DISCLAIMER.

DISCLAIMER

This was a staged production. All persons appearing in this programme, including the audience, are professional actors.

Cue CREDITS.

Host

Maverick Wilson, actor, stage magician, illusionist and hypnotist

Sylvia

Sylvia Silver, porn star/actress (of over 30 adult films)

Sandy

Randy Mellows, actor, former porn star, transsexual gender bender

Jane

Jane Metcalfe, actress, member of RADA

Adam

Adam Stewart, actor, gay activist

Written by

Jon Lange

Casting Director

Erik Weisz

Production Assistant

Peter Perdurabo

Stage Manager

Harry Blackstone

Technical Supervisor

Edward Kelly

Make-Up

Lela Waddell

Costume Designer

Sybil Merlin

Senior Cameraman

Anthony Blake

Sound

Julian Karswell

Lighting

Albert Vogler

Design

Jon D.

Special Effects by

VeverMedia

Produced and Directed by

Oliver Haddo

A Prestigious Production, 2015

Made in the USA
Charleston, SC
14 August 2014